Engelbert Sneem

and his
Dream Vacuum Machine

Written & illustrated by

Mr. Daniel Postgate

NORTHSOUTH
BOOKS

New York

*I*n this world
where we live,
it is really quite sad
That a number of people
grow up to be bad.

We have rascals and robbers
    and cheaters and pinchers
And fibbers and squealers
    and scoundrels and stinkers.
But out of them all
    there is nobody meaner
Than Engelbert Sneem
    and his Dream Vacuum Cleaner.

At night time, when children
    slip into their beds
And onto soft pillows
    they lay their sweet heads,
It isn't too long
    before dreaming begins,
And while they are dreaming
    of wonderful things...
Of fairies and flowers
    and rainbows and kings...

From out of the darkness,

out of the gloom,
Mr. Engelbert Sneem
tip-toes into the room.
And he sucks up their dreams
with his dreadful machine,
Then leaps out the window
before he is seen.

He puts all the dreams
into pottery flagons,
Climbs onto his carriage,
and screams to his dragons,

*"Come open your wings,
pretty lizards, take flight!"*

Then Engelbert Sneem
flies away through the night.

To a Kingdom of permanent
    darkness he flies,
Where a restless and rampaging
    storm fills the skies.
Where rumbling thunder
    and bright lightning flashes
Across a dark sea
    which perpetually crashes
Against a black rock
    on which stands at its peak,

The Castle of Sneem,

oh so silent and bleak.

Down echoing stairs
  goes the burgling rascal,
Dragging his sack
  to the bowels of his castle
Where flagons are stored
  upon old wooden beams...

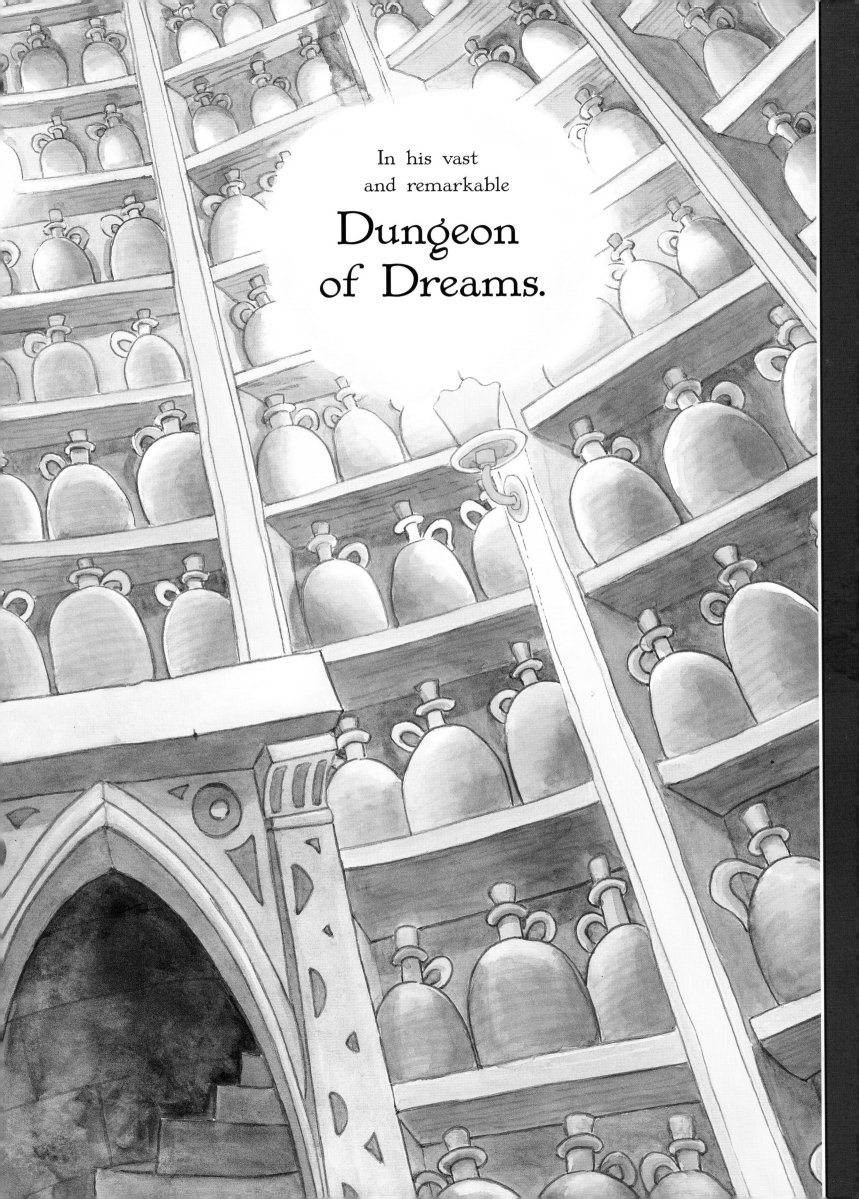

In his vast
and remarkable
Dungeon
of Dreams.

Then if Sneem ever fancies
a nice little treat,
He picks out a flagon
that's sassy and sweet,
He pops out the cork
with the greatest of pleasure,
Then savours a sumptuous
dream at his leisure.

And I very much doubt
whether Sneem's ever wondered
What happens to children
whose dreams he has plundered.
Why, robbed of their dreaming
they grow up to be
Those miserable adults
you so often see.

A little boy said to his mom,
"Is this right?
Is there really a man
who steals dreams every night?"
"Oh, hush now my child,"
said his mom, "take a look!
It is only a tale
in a fairy tale book.

"You sleep now my darling
and have a nice dream."
And he did have a dream,
but the dream was of Sneem.

And while the boy dreamt
of the tale he had read,
A shadowy figure crept up to his bed,
And he sucked up the dream
and he plugged it up tight,
Then he chuckled and
scuttled away through the night.

Once back in his castle,
the crook, with great pleasure,
Pulled out the cork
from his freshly caught treasure.
And as the dream billowed
and swirled through the air,
A shocking and scandalous tale
was laid bare...

The tale of a greedy
and pilfering thief
Who left in his wake
only sadness and grief.
Cried Engelbert Sneem
(for of course it was he)...

"...I've uncorked a nightmare...

...and the nightmare is ME!"

In absolute horror,
  Sneem let out such screams
That they shattered the thousands
  of flagons of dreams.
And all of those wonderful dreams,
  they took flight,
Transforming the darkness
  to sweetness and light.
The sea became calm
  and the sky became blue,
Then up and away
  those most splendid dreams flew...

  Back to the people
  to whom they belong,
Bringing them happiness,
    laughter,
      and song.

Alone, in his throne room,
Sneem pondered his plight
(With just an umbrella
to keep off the light).
He sat and he brooded
for days upon days,
Then finally whispered,

"*I must change my ways.*"

And now...
 if a child
  has frightening dreams
Of ghosties and ghoulies
 and terrible things,

The good Mr. Sneem
 is right there in a tick,
And he sucks up the nightmare
 and plugs it up quick.
Then he carefully writes
 on the flagon with chalk:

'Please
leave this alone,
Do not open
this flagon.

WARNING:
Protected by Dragon!'

And he takes it away
to his dungeon
so then...

That child will never
have nightmares again.

For Harry

Published and distributed in the United States
and Canada in 2007 by North-South Books Inc.,
an imprint of NordSüd Verlag AG, Zürich, Switzerland.

Library of Congress Cataloging-in-Publication Data is available.
A CIP catalogue record for this book is available from The British Library.

ISBN-13: 978-0-7358-2151-4
ISBN-10: 0-7358-2151-8

1 3 5 7 9 10 8 6 4 2

Printed in Belgium